For Skye,

who inspired me to write this book.

A
forest

by Marc Martin

There once was a forest.

Over thousands of years, the forest had grown into thick, lush woodland.

One day, people started cutting down the forest.

At first they only cut down a little, and everything they took from the forest, they replaced.

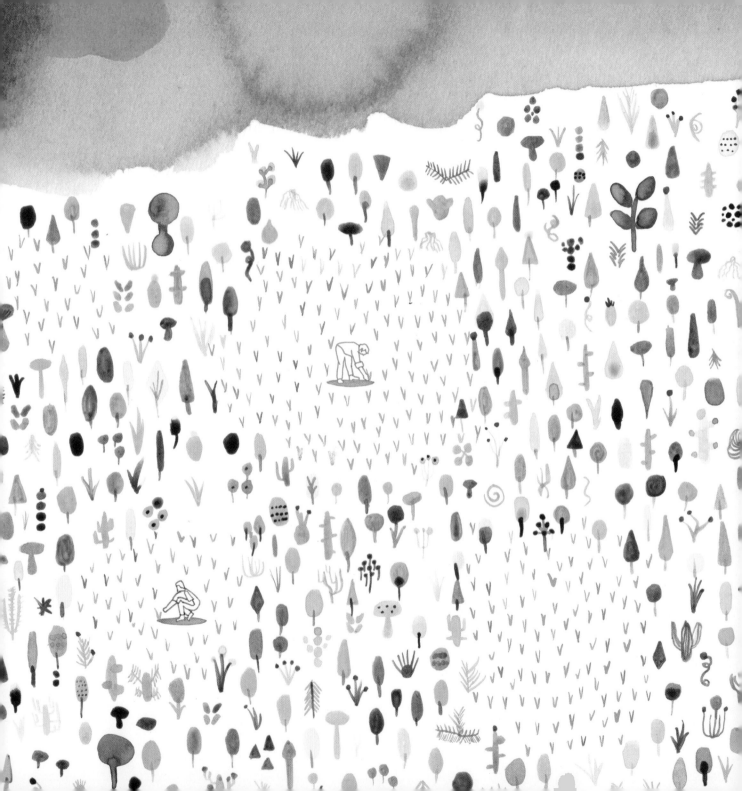

However, they soon became greedy,
and took as much as they could from the forest.

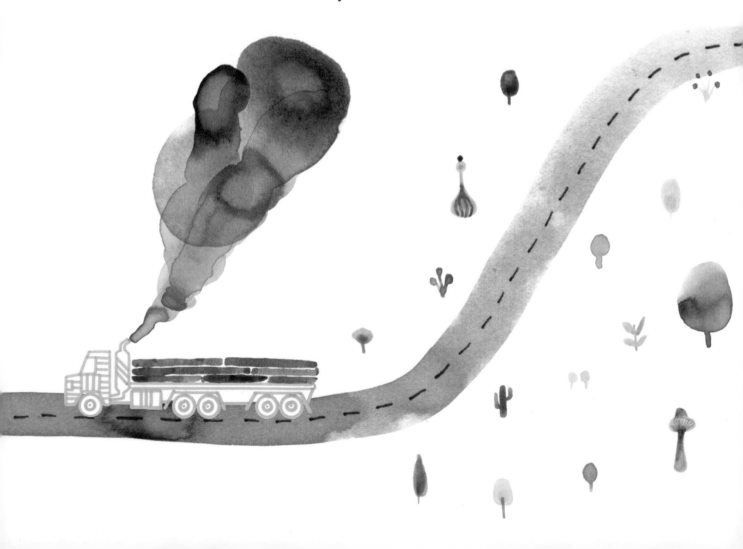

They replaced all the trees with buildings and factories ...

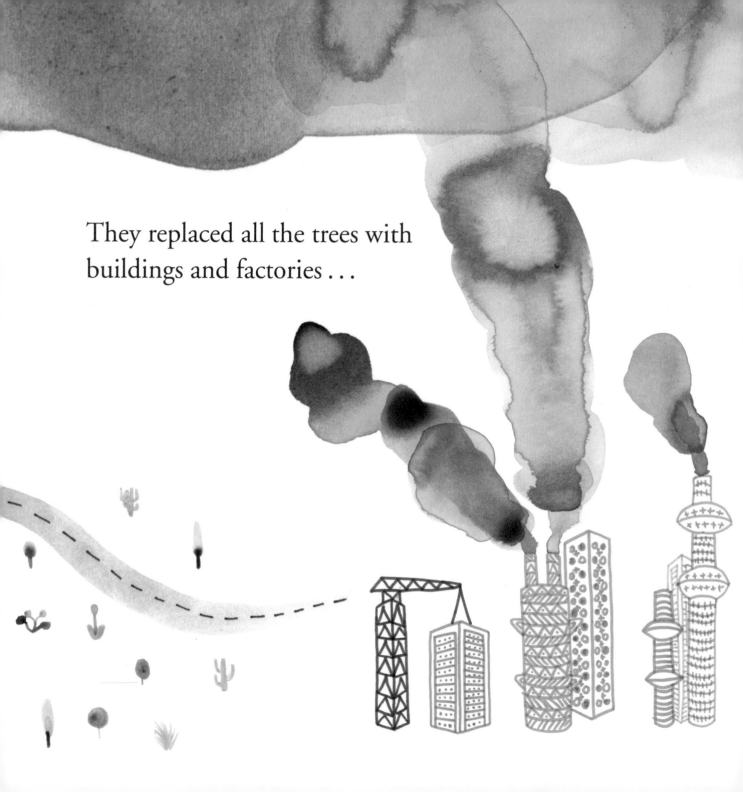

. . . and they built a city.

Yet without the forest to make the air clean,
it became thick and dirty.

The air became so thick that a dreadful
storm began to brew . . .

. . . and it started to rain very strongly.

The rain was so strong that it washed all the buildings away.

When the rain finally stopped,
all that was left was one little tree.

Over time, that one tree became many trees . . .

. . . and soon it became

. . . a forest.

Marc Martin is an award-winning illustrator based in Melbourne,
Australia. Working with a variety of mediums, Marc's work is a
world of dense colour, rich textures and the odd scribble.
More of his artwork can be found at www.marcmartin.com
A Forest is his first picture book.

A TEMPLAR BOOK

This edition first published in the UK in 2015 by Templar Publishing,
an imprint of The Templar Company Limited,
Deepdene Lodge, Deepdene Avenue, Dorking, Surrey, RH5 4AT, UK
www.templarco.co.uk

First published by Penguin Group (Australia), 2012

ISBN 978-1-78370-208-4

Cover and internal design by Marc Martin

Printed in China